Disney's
Winnie the Pooh
Forgive and Forget

When someone says, "I'm sorry!"

And it's really from the heart,

Forgive and forget what happened.

Give your friend a brand-new start!

One spring morning, Rabbit looked around and decided his house needed a good cleaning. He was busy sweeping when he heard a knock at the door. Taking off his apron, he went to answer it.

It was Tigger bouncing by to say hello.

"Hoo-hoo-hoo! Whatcha up to?" asked Tigger playfully.

"I'm busy putting things in order," Rabbit replied. "And I don't have time to stop and chat, Tigger."

"Tsk-tsk! Too bad for you," Tigger muttered under his breath. "Well, I guess I'll be on my way, seeing as how you have no time . . . ," Tigger said. But he couldn't resist playing a joke on Rabbit before he left.

While Rabbit was busy cleaning, Tigger turned back the hands on his clock.

"T-T-F-N! Ta-Ta For Now! See ya later, Long Ears!" called Tigger, chuckling to himself. "Have a good time cleaning!"

Rabbit swept and dusted, polished and mopped, buffed and scrubbed, until his house was shiny and spotless.

"Perfect!" he said, admiring his hard work.

Just then there was another knock at the door.

This time it was Pooh and Christopher Robin, looking
very puzzled.

"Rabbit," said Christopher Robin, "where have you been?
We've been waiting for you for hours to pick flowers."

"Did you forget us, perhaps?" asked Pooh.

"Don't be ridiculous!" replied Rabbit. "Why, it's only noon, and I said I'd meet you at three o'clock."

Christopher Robin looked at his watch.
"Actually, it's almost five o'clock. Time for me to head home for supper," he said. "Sorry, Rabbit."

Rabbit looked at his clock on the mantel.
He held it up to his ear and listened—it seemed to be
ticking just fine. How had it lost so much time?

"Tigger!" Rabbit suddenly exclaimed. "I'll bet he played a prank on me and turned back the clock!"
Rabbit was angry.

"Oh, dear," said Pooh, trying to calm him down. "I'm sure Tigger was just having some fun. Besides, there's always tomorrow for picking flowers."

But Rabbit didn't want to forgive Tigger.
Instead, he stomped off in search of him. Rabbit found Tigger
bouncing happily in the Wood.

"Say, isn't it a little late for an afternoon stroll, Rabbit?" Tigger joked.

"Not funny," harumphed Rabbit. "I think I know what you did to my clock, and it ruined my whole day!"

The next day, Tigger felt so bad that he went over to Rabbit's house to apologize.

"I'm sorry, Rabbit Ol' Pal," he said. "Didn't mean to get your fur all ruffled!"

Rabbit turned away as if Tigger wasn't even there.
And no matter how many times Tigger said he was sorry,
Rabbit refused to forgive and forget what he'd done.

The next day, Tigger and Roo stopped by to offer Rabbit some fresh carrot cake that Kanga, Tigger, and Roo had baked. Carrot cake was Rabbit's favorite.

"If it comes from a certain tigger, I'm not hungry," said Rabbit.

"But Rabbit," Roo urged him, "Tigger said he was sorry. Won't you forgive and forget? Don't you want just a little piece of cake?"

"Absolutely not!" said Rabbit firmly, even though he *was* a bit hungry.

Later, Tigger and Piglet offered to help Rabbit hang new curtains in his window.

"I'll bounce up and hang them in a jifferoo!" offered Tigger.

"I can do it myself," insisted Rabbit, huffing and puffing.

That evening Pooh and Tigger went over to Rabbit's house.
"Rabbit, I think Tigger is very sorry," Pooh said. "Won't
you forgive and forget?"
"Apologies," sniffed Rabbit, "just won't do."

No matter how much everyone urged Rabbit to forgive Tigger,
he wouldn't change his mind.

Then one rainy day, Rabbit was heading across a bridge when
a strong gust of wind knocked him into the stream.

"Help! Help!" cried Rabbit.

Tigger heard his cries and quickly came to the rescue.

"Don't you worry, Rabbit," said Tigger, tugging him safely ashore. "We tiggers are expert swimmers, you know!"

"Phew," said Tigger, panting. "That was a close one."

Rabbit looked at Tigger, who was sopping wet. Rabbit knew that only a good friend would jump into the stream to save him. At that moment, Rabbit decided to forgive Tigger.

When the sun came out the next day, Rabbit whipped up a crunchy salad and invited everyone to help him eat it.
Tigger watched sadly as his friends dug in.
Surely Rabbit wouldn't want to share with him!

But to Tigger's surprise, Rabbit made an announcement.
"I owe this delicious meal to my friend Tigger," said Rabbit.
Then he handed Tigger a big bowl of salad. "*Forgive and
forget*, that's what I always say . . . ," shouted Rabbit.

"I forgive you, Tigger," Rabbit continued. "But there's one thing I'll never forget: what a good friend you were to rescue me. Thank you!"

And with that, everyone gave three great big cheers for both Tigger and Rabbit.

A LESSON A DAY POOH'S WAY

A friend

always forgives

and forgets.